JUNETEENTH

Celebrating Freedom

Written and Illustrated by

Julian Van Dyke

To order additional copies of this book, contact:
Xlibris
1-888-795-4274
www.Xlibris.com
Orders@Xlibris.com

ISBN: Softcover   978-1-7960-9928-7
          EBook   978-1-7960-9927-0

Print information available on the last page

Rev. date: 04/23/2020

Juneteenth,

Celebrating Freedom

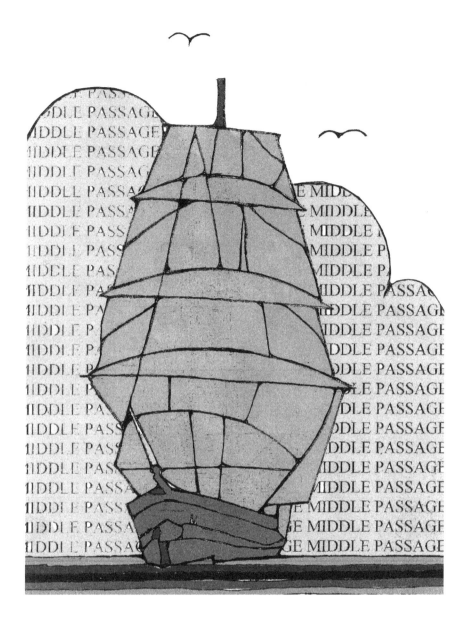

We must remember that slavery has been in the world since the dawn of man. Even in Africa, slaves were people captured in war, or those who sold themselves to sustain their life or starvation.

But as time went by in the world the demand for slaves grew at a massive scale. Many of our ancestors did not live through the Middle Passage across the Atlantic Ocean. A trade network had been established with people as cargo that linked Africa, Europe and the Americas.

JUNETEENTH

On June 19, 1865 in Galveston, Texas Our ancestors celebrated the delayed communication of the end of the Civil War and the enforcement of the Emancipation Proclamation. This renowned celebration became known as Juneteenth, the oldest known celebration for the ending of slavery. Since this spontaneous celebration, the Juneteenth holiday has spread across the country by many African Americans families. Although Juneteenth is a time for celebration, it is also a time to honor and give patronage to our ancestors and the struggles of African American slaves during this difficult and challenging time in history. It will never be known how many teachers, artists and doctors were lost during this time period. It is vitally important to recognize and remember the Juneteenth holiday and to ensure that history does not repeat itself and future generations continue to work together to ensure a brighter tomorrow.

We celebrate with lessons and stories told from old.

Of times when we were kings and queens, and warriors were bold.

We celebrate by reading General Order number three. The Proclamation that declared that all slaves to be free

We celebrate with cheering, and with spiritual songs. Giving praise unto the Lord who brought us all along.

We celebrate remembering of those who were enslaved. To honor those who lost their lives so freedom could be paved.

We celebrate with singing and music in the shade.

Songs sung by church choirs…

...and bands marching in parades.

We celebrate our freedom with picnics in parks.

With family reunions..

..Until way after dark.

We play baseball, softball and sack races too.

And couples play "Cakewalk" to just name a few.

With barbecue cook offs...

And blessings of food..

...That places the day in a fun festive mood.

Listening to poets and art work to see...

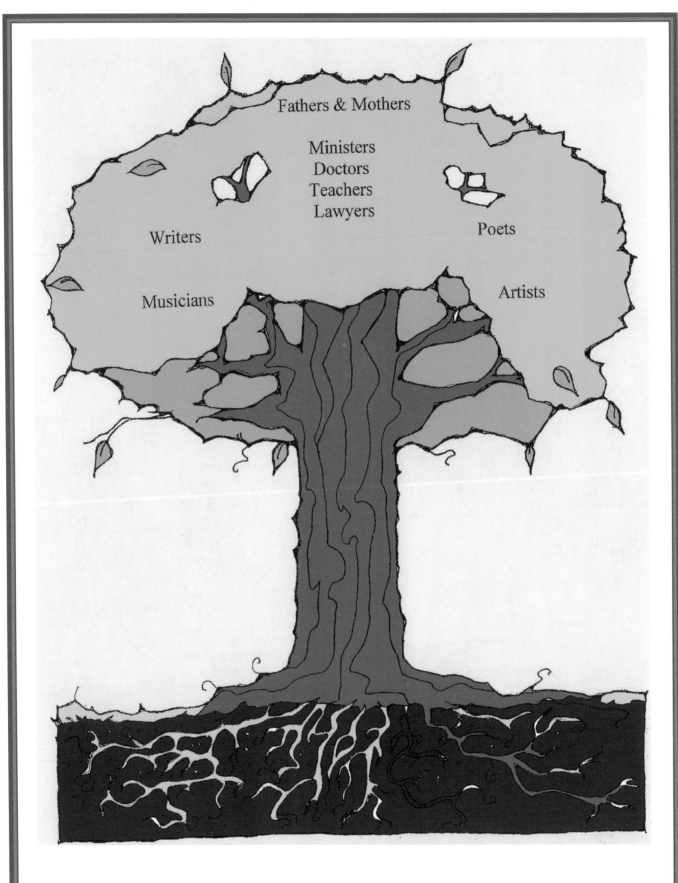

...Helping to save our own legacy

Giving thanks to those who have gone through great lengths, and celebrate the joy and time of Juneteenth!

CPSIA information can be obtained
at www.ICGtesting.com
Printed in the USA
BVHW021436220621
610209BV00009B/350